What Is Miss Green?

BY Suzanne McNail

DORRANCE
PUBLISHING CO
EST. 1920
PITTSBURGH, PENNSYLVANIA 15238

Dorrance Publishing Co
585 Alpha Drive, Suite 103
Pittsburgh, PA 15238
Visit our website at www.dorrancebookstore.com

ISBN: 978-1-4809-2503-8
eISBN: 978-1-4809-2273-0

For Jim, Norah, and Brady.

You teach me life's greatest lessons.

Shout

Hocus-Pocus

when you spot Miss Green's broom glow
and see what strange events happen next!

Brady's Journal:

Miss Green is my teacher—
very different from the rest.
She is not like other teachers,
she has magic, I suspect!

When she enters the room, her presence is known.
I feel the chills zing through my bones!

From her bright red hair and crooked nose,
to her long bony fingers and pointy toes...

...she looks quite enchanting in her own way,
and wears a fancy new hat for every school day.

Some dressed in feathers, some wrapped with lace,
one had a raven perched in place!

Once, I saw the principal sneak away her closet key, and open the door to find the most unusual things—dozens of potions with wispy vapors;

and was that a black cat grading our papers?
What happened next was really weird,
my principal just disappeared!

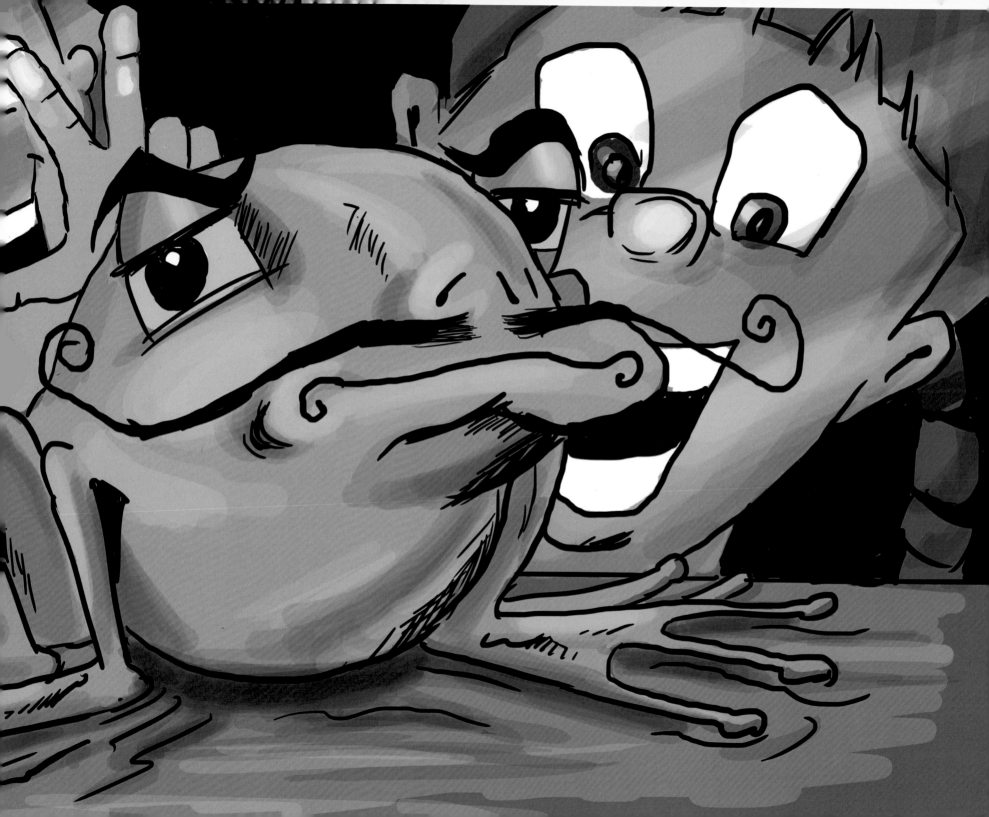

At the science fair we took first place
for blasting our class frog into outer space;

and don't dare make silly faces
when you think she can't see,
or else your face may stick that way
for a day or three!

Like science, math, and history,
even our spelling bee is a mystery.
Is it a spelling bee or a bee of spells?
The words I spelled I could not tell!

At lunch she gobbles up her creature stew
that is made up of her homemade brew—
a mix of toads, crickets, and snails,
she loudly slurps up lizards' tails.

SMACK! A lizard tail whipped her cheek
and left a trail with a glowing gleam.
When she tried to wipe it clean,
she wiped her cheek and it turned green!

At twelve o'clock, the raven cries, "AWK!"
It's time to go out for recess.
The students trample out the door
and leave behind a horrid mess.

I did not go out to play,
I must see what she is TODAY!

I peer through the window, and what do I see?
What I see next I can't believe!

She calls out to the closet that holds her broom,
"Come out, my friend, and clean this room!"

Out flies the broom in a hasty gust,
sweeping the floor clean of dust.

With a snap of her fingers and twitch of her nose,
a tornado of the clutter arose!

The pencils and books swarm into their places,
with one sweep of her hand the desks march to their spaces!

She twirls in the air around and around,
as her pointy toes never touch the ground!

She turns her head to glance at me with a smile and a wink.

At this moment, I do think . . .
Miss Green is a teacher who is *magically unique!*

What strange events
happened when you shouted

Hocus-Pocus?

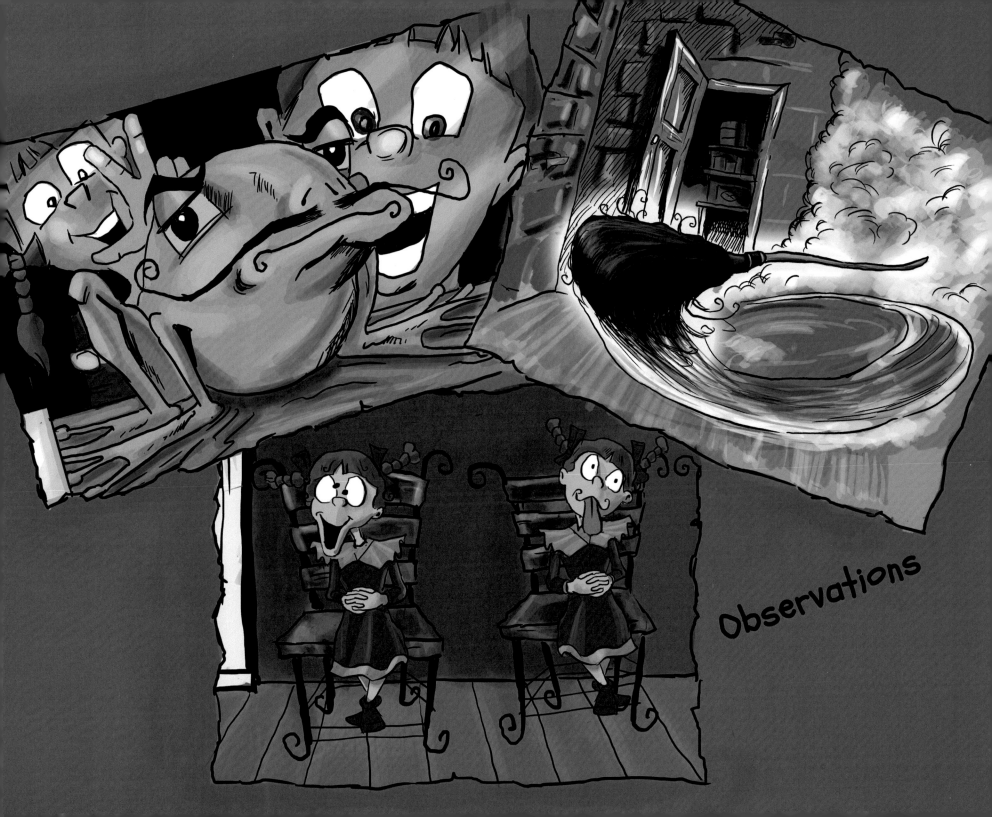

Observations